HISTORY QUIC

VICTORIAN BRITAIN

The Castle Builder
Daisy's Diary
The Runaway

by Stephanie Baudet

Illustrated by Robin Lawrie

ANGLIA *a* BOOKS
young

First published in 2003
by Anglia Young Books

Anglia Young Books is an imprint of
Mill Publishing Ltd
PO Box 120
Bangor
County Down BT19 7BX

Illustrations by Robin Lawrie
Design by Angela Ashton

British Library Cataloguing-in-Publication Data

A catalogue record for this book is available from the British Library

ISBN 1 871173 87 6

Printed in Great Britain by Ashford Colour Press, Gosport, Hampshire

CONTENTS

THE CASTLE BUILDER

Tom's mother stood by the cottage door. She watched Tom set off in the pony-and-cart.

'Good luck, son,' she called.

The cart rattled along the track towards Crathie.

Tom was twelve and it was time for him to find work. Their small sheep farm could not support his big family. He must find other work with his pony and cart.

He stopped when he reached the old castle of Balmoral. A big space had been cleared and he saw men unloading blocks of stone from wagons.

What was going on?

Tom drove the cart through the castle gates. He saw a man having a rest beside a wagon.

'What's happening?' asked Tom.

'We are building a new castle for Queen Victoria,' said the man.

'Do you need some help?' asked Tom.

The man laughed. He pointed to the wagon. 'These are granite blocks from Glen Gelder quarry,' he said. 'They are too heavy for your pony.'

'My pony's strong,' said Tom. 'We can fetch one block at a time.'

'Go and see the foreman, then,' said the man.

The foreman was telling some men what to do. They were taking the blocks from the wagons and putting them in a big pile.

'Please sir,' said Tom. 'I need some work.'

The foreman looked at Tom and laughed. But Tom kept on asking.

'*Please* sir! My pony is strong. We can fetch one block at a time.'

At last the foreman promised Tom one <u>penny</u> for each block delivered.

'But if you damage a block, you will be fined threepence,' he said.

'Thank you, sir,' said Tom.

Glen Gelder quarry was only a mile away. Tom set off in his pony-and-cart.

As he urged his pony through the river, he looked back at the old castle. It had been there for hundreds of years. Now there would be a new one, built specially for Queen Victoria.

When he reached the quarry, there was a lot of noise. Men were breaking the granite with picks and huge steam cranes hissed as they lifted the blocks onto wagons.

As soon as Tom's block was loaded, he set off back to the castle. One penny per block. He must make as many trips as possible.

But when Tom reached the river with his heavy load, the cart got stuck.

The cart tipped up. The block of stone could slide out at any moment!

Tom jumped out into the water. He looked at the wheel. It was stuck between two rocks. His pony was nervous and broke its harness.

Tom patted the pony's neck and stroked its ears. 'Calm down boy,' he said. 'It's all right.'

But Tom didn't feel calm himself. What should he do? If the block fell into the river, he would have to pay threepence. The men from the castle would have to come and help him. They would laugh at him.

Tom blinked back the tears. He had let his family down. Instead of earning money, he was losing it.

He was so upset that he didn't hear the woman come up behind him.

'Are you all right?' she said.

Tom jumped and looked round. He saw a lady standing on the bank. She was dressed in fine clothes.

'No, Ma'am,' said Tom. 'I was to earn a penny for each block of granite I fetched from the quarry. Now, my cart is stuck and the pony's harness is broken.'

'I'm sorry to hear that, young man,' she said. 'What is your name?'

Tom could tell that the lady was a stranger. She didn't speak like a local person.

'My name is Tom McNabb, Ma'am,' said Tom.

The lady smiled. 'Well, you wait here with your pony, Tom McNabb,' she said. 'I shall go and find some help.'

Then she turned and walked away. When she reached a corner in the track, she waved back at him. Tom watched as the sunlight sparkled on the rings on her fingers.

Tom waited patiently with his pony. The sun moved across the sky. It was getting late.

The pony was restless. Suddenly there was a grinding noise as the cart moved and the block of granite slid towards the edge.

Any minute it would land in the river!

Tom didn't know what to do. If he unhitched the pony from the cart, the cart would tip, then the granite would slip off.

'I expect the rich lady has forgotten all about me,' Tom thought. 'I shall have to stay here in the cold water until someone else comes along.'

He bit his lip. He was near to tears.

Suddenly he heard the sound of a horse's hooves and of men's voices.

Six men were leading a big horse down the track.

'Hello Tom,' they said. 'We've come to help you.'

How did they know his name?

The men steadied the granite block. Then they unhitched Tom's pony and hitched up the big horse to Tom's cart.

'Come on, Brownie, pull hard,' they shouted.

With a heave, the wheel was freed and the big horse pulled the cart out of the river.

'We'll take your pony back to the stables for you,' said one of the men. 'The Queen says you can borrow Brownie for as long as you like.'

'The Queen?' gasped Tom.

The men laughed at the look on his face. One of them handed Brownie's reins to Tom.

'Her Majesty says we must help you with your work. She wants her new castle built as quickly as possible. Tomorrow she will lay the

<u>foundation stone</u> and she wishes you to be there.'

Tom took the reins. He couldn't believe it! The rich lady who spoke to him must have been the Queen! Queen Victoria herself!

At last, he found his voice. 'Thank you very much, sir,' he said. 'I shall be there.'

The next day, dressed in his best, Tom stood and watched Queen Victoria lay the mortar for the foundation stone. When she had finished, she turned and looked at the small crowd watching. When she saw Tom, she smiled and waved.

Flashes of light sparkled and danced from the rings on her fingers.

Historical Notes
for The Castle Builder 1853

In 1852 Queen Victoria and her husband, Prince Albert, went on holiday to Scotland. They stayed in the old Balmoral Castle which was built in the 15th century. She loved it so much that Prince Albert bought it for her as a present. It cost £32,000.

They decided to build a new castle which would be more comfortable than the draughty old one. It is built of white granite from Glen Gelder quarry nearby. Prince Albert paid for it out of his own money.

In 1853 the building started and Queen Victoria laid the foundation stone. The castle was finished in 1855. Then the old castle was knocked down.

Queen Victoria loved rings and would wear a lot of them at the same time. She also liked to go around like an ordinary person and hope that she wouldn't be recognised.

Glossary

- <u>granite</u> – a very hard sort of rock.

- <u>penny</u> – one old penny. There were twelve pennies to a shilling and twenty shillings to a pound.

- <u>foundation stone</u> – when an important building is begun, a famous person is asked to lay one of the first building blocks. They don't have to lift the block. They lay the mortar and, when the block is in place, they make a speech.

DAISY'S DIARY

Sunday 7ᵗʰ September 1856

Today I left the <u>workhouse</u>. I'm not going back, either. Ever. Mind, when I got here this afternoon I was so scared I nearly turned round and ran.

The house is so grand! And the trees! Ever so high they are. I never knew there were such big trees in London.

It is a rich people's street all right. Me in my only dress, with a torn <u>bodice</u>. It split when I sat down on the <u>omnibus</u>.

This diary is what Pa gave me before he went to fight in that war in the Crimea. He came back wounded and then died. I never wrote anything in the workhouse. There was nothing to tell. Now there will be plenty.

Pa said be thankful for what you have, but try to get what you want out of life. He wrote in my diary, on the first page. It says 'Seek much and get something, seek little and get nothing.'

I do miss Pa.

I found number 65. Big pillars at the front door and a shining brass knocker. 'Course I knew not to go to the front door. I ain't daft. I went to the kitchen door.

It was the cook who opened it. A big lady with a red face and a thin mouth. Here's a strict one, I thought.

She told me to come in and sit down. Then she gave me a cup of tea and said it was the last time I'd be waited on.

Monday 8th September 1856

I couldn't finish yesterday's diary because *she* complained about me burning the candle when she was trying to sleep.

Florence her name is. She's the parlourmaid and doesn't like her name shortened. I learnt that much.

I was set straight to work yesterday. I get £8 a year. That's three shillings a week, all found! I've got a nice black dress, a white apron and a cap. I can keep them if I stay a year. We get good meals. Meat and two vegetables *and* a pudding. I'll get fat!

Florence is getting really cross so I'll have to stop. She says I think I'm better than them because I can read and write. She says the master, Colonel Watkinson, wouldn't like it. Servants should know their place. Even Cook can only read and write enough to order food.

Well, I remember what Pa said. You can't get on in the world if you can't read and write. I learned in the workhouse school.

Tuesday 9th September 1856

I'm in the kitchen sitting by the <u>range</u>. Cook said I could stay here just as long as my candle lasted out. It's nice and warm here. Our attic has no fireplace but we have three blankets on our beds. It's not a bad room. There's a <u>washstand</u> and a wardrobe though I've nothing to put in it.

Wednesday 10th September 1856

I haven't met the master and mistress and don't expect I shall. They never come into the kitchen and I never go into the main house. I would love to see it though.

My hands are so sore I can hardly write. It's having them in water all day, Cook says. There's <u>soda</u> in it to get the dishes clean. She says they'll harden up soon. They're red and cracked and two fingers are bleeding. They were too sore to do much scouring today because we use sand and ginger to get them copper pans clean.

If there's any candle left after writing the diary I read my book. It's called *Holiday House* by Catherine Sinclair. Ma gave it to me so I value it. I only have three things I own. My book, my diary and Pa's war medal. How can you lose everything in three years?

I'd give anything to go back. Before Pa went to war. Before the typhoid got Ma and my three sisters. Before the workhouse.

Thursday 11th September 1856

That Florence has got me in trouble. She's a spiteful one. She broke a china vase while she was dusting and blamed me! She said I was in the main house, where I shouldn't be. She said I told her I wanted to see the house. She said I picked up the vase and then dropped it.

It's all lies. Except the bit about wanting to see the house.

Tomorrow I am being sent to the mistress, Mrs Watkinson. Florence says she'll dismiss me. She says it serves me right for being high and mighty, and reading and writing won't do me no good.

Friday 12th September 1856

I'd never been so scared in all my life. At ten o'clock Mrs Watkinson sent for me. I went up the back stairs to her room.

She was nice, the mistress was, but she said she didn't like servants who broke the rules and she would have to let me go.

Go where with no <u>references</u>? Back to the workhouse.

I didn't speak I was so choked up. I didn't say it wasn't me that broke the vase. She is sure to believe Florence.

When I got out of the room I couldn't hold back my tears any longer. I didn't see where I was going and started down the main stairs without knowing it. Then I fell and tumbled all the way down.

I hurt all over and couldn't get my breath back. Then a voice said, 'My dear child, are you hurt?'

I looked up and a bald-headed man with a large moustache was bending over me. It must be Colonel Watkinson, I thought, and tried to get up quickly.

'Careful,' he said. 'You may have broken something.' Then he gasped and took hold of Pa's medal which I always wear round my neck.

'Where did you get this?' he asked.

'It was Pa's, sir,' I whispered.

'What was your Pa's name?'

'Henry Barton, sir.'

Then the Colonel helped me to stand up and sat me on a chair in the hall. He asked me who I was and what had happened and I told him the whole story.

Then he told me that he had known Pa. He had been Pa's Commanding Officer. He told me how brave Pa had been in the war and I should be proud of him.

Then he took me upstairs and told the whole story to his wife.

Saturday 13th September 1856

I'm writing this in my room again. Florence has been dismissed and I have her job.

Colonel and Mrs Watkinson are really nice.
They say they don't agree with people who
want their servants to stay illiterate. (That's not
being able to read or write. It's a new word
I learned today.) They say I can go to evening
school one or two times a week if I want.
I reckon they are really good employers and
I'm very lucky.

Thanks Pa.

Historical Notes
for Daisy's Diary 1856

In Victorian times many people had servants.
Even ordinary working people often had one
servant. The richer you were, the more you
had. Some large country houses had over three
hundred. A scullery maid like Daisy was a very
low position. Her job was to wash and scrub
dishes and pans, to help prepare vegetables and
to clean the kitchen.

Lower servants had very little free time. They
worked about 18 hours a day. Some had half a
day off a month. They usually shared a small

attic room and were given a uniform and all meals.

The Crimean War (1853 to 1856) was fought against Russia by Britain, France, Turkey and Sardinia. The Crimea is a part of Russia which sticks out into the Black Sea.

As well as thousands of men dying in battle, many more thousands died of cold, starvation and cholera. You can also read about *The Charge of the Light Brigade* and *Florence Nightingale*.

Daisy's mother and sisters died of typhoid. Like cholera, this is a disease which is caused by polluted water. There was no proper sewerage system so that human waste got into the drinking water. In 1859 an engineer called *Joseph Bazalgette* began building sewers under the streets of London. When they were finished in 1873 there were 82 miles of sewers. These were so well built that they are still used today. Now the sewage is treated to make it clean.

In those days it just went into the Thames and down to the sea.

Glossary

- workhouse – a place which gave food and shelter to very poor people. They had very strict rules and separated males and females, including children.

- bodice – the top half of a dress.

- omnibus – a horse-drawn bus which could hold about twenty people.

- parlourmaid – a servant who dusts and cleans the house.

- shilling – before decimal money there were twenty shillings in a pound and twelve pence in a shilling.

- all found – everything provided: meals, room and uniform.

- range – a big fuel-burning cooker.

- washstand – a table with a water jug and a basin to wash in.

- soda – washing soda was a sort of salt (sodium carbonate) used for washing dishes and clothes.

- reference – a letter to tell your next employer how well you did your work.

THE RUNAWAY

Will was miserable at boarding school so he ran away. He hid in a cart.

The journey was long and uncomfortable. Then the cart stopped in a strange part of London.

Will got out but he didn't know where he was. It was getting late. He was lost and very scared.

He walked for a long time. The streets were crowded and the smell was terrible. People pushed and shoved. There was mud and animal pee everywhere. Soon his uniform was filthy and his shoes were soaked.

Will bent down and took off his shoes. He put them on a wall to dry them out.

Suddenly, a ragged, barefoot boy pushed him over and grabbed his shoes from the wall.

'Hey!' shouted Will. 'Give me back my shoes!'

Will was too angry to be scared. He jumped up and ran after the boy, dodging in and out of the crowds. The boy ran fast, but Will was faster. Then the boy tripped on a stone and fell.

Will sat on top of him. 'Give me my shoes,' he gasped.

'Let me get up then,' said the boy. Will let go and the boy stood up. He flung the shoes at Will. He was about to run off again, but then he stopped and frowned.

'You're a toff!' he said. 'You don't belong here!'

Will didn't answer. He put on his wet shoes.

'Where have you come from?' asked the boy. 'Have you run away?'

'None of your business,' muttered Will.

The boy looked at Will's uniform. 'You've run away from school, haven't you?'

Will didn't answer.

'My name's Jack,' said the boy. 'What's yours?'

'Will,' said Will. He felt very alone. He sniffed and rubbed his eyes. He must not cry in front of this street boy.

Jack grinned suddenly. 'You hungry?'

Will nodded.

'Stay here then. I'll get something to eat.'

Soon Jack was back carrying a hot pie in his dirty hands. He gave half the pie to Will.

'I can't pay for it,' said Will.

Jack grinned. 'Nor can I,' he said. 'I stole it from the <u>pieman</u>.' He stuffed his piece of pie into his mouth. Gravy ran down his chin.

'But stealing's wrong!'

Jack glared at him. 'You'd steal if you were starving,' he said.

Will bit into his pie. He'd never been so hungry. He looked at Jack's thin body. Jack was probably hungry every day.

Jack finished his pie. 'You want somewhere to sleep?' he said.

Will nodded.

He followed Jack down dark alleys to the railway line. Jack showed him a pile of coal sacks under a bridge.

Will stared. 'Haven't you got a house?' he said.

Jack shook his head. 'I lived with my Ma in one room. Then they knocked the house down.'

'Who knocked it down?'

'The people who built the railway. They knocked down hundreds of houses,' said Jack. 'They promised us somewhere to live, but nothing happened.'

'Where's your Ma then?'

'In the <u>workhouse</u>,' said Jack.

Just then a train thundered over the bridge. Steam and smoke swirled around them.

'Why did you run away?' asked Jack, when the noise had died away.

Will sighed. 'It's hard for me to learn to read,' he said. 'I get the words mixed up and the teachers hit my hands with a cane and beat me with a strap. All the boys tease me.'

'Why don't you tell your Pa?'

'You don't know him,' said Will grimly. 'He wouldn't understand.'

'I'm going to learn to read and write,' said Jack. 'They teach you for free at the Ragged School in Whitechapel.' Then he went on. 'That's why I wanted some shoes. You don't *have* to have shoes to go there, but I don't want to go to school in bare feet.'

The two boys lay down. Jack was used to the noise and smoke and was soon asleep. Will stayed wide awake.

Suddenly he felt a kick in his side. Two men were leaning over him. He could smell their stinking breath. A lantern lit up their faces.

'What have we here?' said one. He was grinning. He had rotten teeth.

'A rich schoolboy with money in his pockets,' said the other.

Will was so scared, he couldn't move. Just then, Jack woke up. 'Clear off!' he shouted.

'Oh it's young Jack, is it? Who's your rich friend?'

One of the men put his hand round Will's throat.

'Come on, empty your pockets,' he hissed.

Jack sprang to his feet. 'He's got no money!' he shouted. 'Leave us alone!'

The man let go of Will and pushed Jack down. Then he spat on the ground and both men walked away into the darkness.

It was a long time before Will stopped shaking.

In the morning, Will asked Jack to help him find his way home.

'You going to tell your Pa then?'

Will nodded. He told Jack the address.

'Yeah, I know where it is,' he said slowly. 'Where toffs live.'

They walked for a long time that morning but at last they reached Will's house. Jack looked up at the smart front door.

'Come in with me,' said Will.

Jack shook his head.

'Please, Jack.'

They went to the back door and into the kitchen. The cook was there. She let out a cry when she saw Will.

'Oh, Master William! Thank heaven you're safe. Your father is so worried. A message has just come from the school. I've never seen him in such a state. Go up and see him straight away, there's a good boy.'

Will nodded. 'Please give my friend some breakfast,' he said. He turned to Jack.

'Don't go away,' he said. 'Wait here.'

Will's heart thumped as he climbed the stairs.

For a moment his father looked glad but then his face went red. His mouth was a thin line. Will knew that look.

'This is a disgrace!' said his father.

Quickly, Will began to talk. At last he told his father how hard it was to learn to read and write. How the teachers hit him instead of helping him. How the other boys teased him. He told his father he couldn't bear it any longer.

When he'd finished, his father was quiet for a moment. Then he nodded.

'My brother was the same,' he said gently. 'He was bullied at school, too.'

He got up and put a hand on Will's shoulder. 'I will get you a private tutor,' he said. 'So you can have special help.'

Then Will told him about Jack. 'Come and meet him,' he said.

So they went down to the kitchen together.

Jack was still eating, but he jumped up when Will and his father came in.

'Thank you for helping my son,' said Will's father.

Will knelt down and took off his shoes. He handed them to Jack.

'I want you to have these,' he said.

Jack took them and grinned. 'Now I can go to school.'

Will smiled back. 'Yes,' he said. 'And I can *leave* school!'

Historical Notes
for The Runaway 1869

Boys from rich families went to boarding school. This cost about £20 a year. There was a lot of bullying by teachers and pupils. If you did not learn, you were hit with a cane or strap. Teachers did not understand that some children find it difficult to learn.

Girls went to academies and learned drawing, music, maths and French. Or they stayed at home and learned to sing and play the piano and to draw and do embroidery. Girls never learned the same subjects as boys.

There were several schools for poorer children.

Dame Schools were run by an older woman. She would charge about four pence a week and would teach reading and writing. Often she was just a child-minder and sometimes children would escape while she slept in a chair!

Common Day Schools charged about nine pence per week. They taught reading, writing, maths, history and geography. Children who attended these schools could then get jobs in shops or offices.

Sunday Schools sometimes taught the children to read and write. Often they just had to learn parts of the Bible by heart without understanding the meaning.

Ragged Schools were free and were for the very poorest children, often those who lived on the streets. They were started in 1818 by a cobbler called John Pounds. In 1844 the Ragged School Union was formed and *Lord Shaftesbury* was the President.

Children were taught reading, writing and arithmetic and boys sometimes learned shoemaking, wood-chopping or other things to help them earn a living. Ragged schools sometimes provided food and somewhere to sleep.

Dr Barnardo also spent his life helping poor children to earn a living and opening Homes where they could live.

In 1880 a law was passed that all children under ten had to go to school.

Railways – Between 1853 and 1883 56,000 people in London lost their homes because of the railways. Most of these people already lived in very crowded homes, often whole families in one room.

After the main city stations were built, the railway companies had to buy all the surrounding land to build the lines, bridges, sheds and coal bunkers. This meant that hundreds of houses had to be knocked down. The rail companies were supposed to build new ones. Often they did not, or the houses they built were so expensive that the poorer people could not afford the rent.

Glossary

- toff – a name for a rich gentleman.

- pieman – a street seller who made and sold different sorts of pie.

- workhouse – a place where really poor people could stay and be fed. The rules were very strict and males and females were separated, including children.